The Fabulous Cakes of

Zinnia Jakes

The Tumbling Tortoises

For Michael, who keeps my dreams alight.

NEW FRONTIER PUBLISHING

First published in Great Britain in 2020
by New Frontier Publishing Europe Ltd.,
Uncommon, 126 New King's Road, London SW6 4LZ

www.newfrontierpublishing.co.uk

ISBN: 978-1-912858-90-3

Illustrated by Nancy Leschnikoff
Text copyright © Brenda Gurr, 2020
Illustrations copyright © New Frontier Publishing, 2020

Edited by Stephanie Stahl
Designed by Rachel Lawston

A CIP catalogue record for this book
is available from the British Library.

Printed and bound in China

The paper and board used in this book
are made from wood from responsible sources.

1 3 5 7 9 10 8 6 4 2

The Fabulous Cakes of
Zinnia  Jakes

The Tumbling Tortoises

Brenda Gurr

Chapter 1

Zoe looked at her lollipop watch for the millionth time and drummed her fingers on her desk. Why hadn't Dad rung yet? She'd sent him a message over an hour ago. Now it was well past bedtime. She checked that her ScreenTouch wasn't on silent and then pressed the home button. A pair of golden cat eyes filled the screen. She grinned. Coco was always taking selfies and changing Zoe's home screen photo when she wasn't looking. The eyes had a fleck of mischief in them, just as they did in real life! Taking selfies was just one of many surprising things that Coco did. It had been three years since she had magically appeared on Aunty Jam's doorstep in the middle of the night. Zoe could still remember the first time she'd met Coco. After she'd wondered aloud what Jam ought to call her new cat, she'd watched as Coco had elegantly traced her name in a patch of sand. Zoe had thought she was imagining things. But now she knew better. Coco was certainly not an ordinary cat!

An ice cream van jingle sounded – Zoe's new ringtone. *Dad!* She hurriedly swiped the screen. She had the best news to tell him!

A video image popped up, showing a man in front of a white domed building. It shone in the bright sunlight. Zoe squinted at the screen. The man, with his shoulder-length blond hair and thick glasses, didn't look at all like her dad. But she wasn't surprised. Dad was often in disguise. In everyday life he was Avery Jones – international food writer. His reviews of restaurants were wildly famous. For the past few years, everyone had been desperate to find out who he was. But Zoe's dad was an expert at going unnoticed. The bad thing about his job was that he was often away. It would probably be at least another month before he would make it home again this time.

'Hi, Dad!' She waved at him. Coco bounded onto the table in front of her, blocking half of the screen. Zoe nudged her to one side.

He smiled. 'Hola, Zoe! Hi there, Coco. Sorry it's taken me so long to call. Bad signal here! What's the big news?'

'I heard back from Wildside Zoo!' said Zoe excitedly.

Dad caught his breath. 'And?'

'I won!' Zoe squealed. She struck a pose. 'I'm the official cake maker for the zoo's endangered animals campaign!' She jiggled about, making the desk shake. Coco stumbled and flattened her ears.

'Wow, Zo, that's awesome! I'm so happy for you!'

'Thanks, Dad,' said Zoe. 'I can't believe it. The best bakers in the whole city entered!'

'*I* believe it,' said Dad firmly. 'I knew you had an excellent chance when I saw your design. Galapagos tortoise cupcakes were a wonderful idea.'

Zoe nodded vigorously, her plaits bouncing. There were so many endangered animals she could have chosen. But the moment she had laid eyes on a photograph of a Galapagos tortoise, she had fallen in love with its wise face and gentle appearance. She'd had so much fun drawing the cupcake design, although it had been a lot of hard work too.

'I can't wait to start making the cupcakes!' she cheered and Dad gave her a big smile.

It was an exciting chance to help save endangered animals. The zoo campaign was big news – many classes from schools in and around the city were getting involved by learning about endangered animals and raising money for them. That included Zoe's own class at Mount Rumbling Primary School. Zoe's cupcakes would be unveiled at the official campaign launch at the zoo the following week.

Dad wiped his brow.

'Is it hot in Argentina?' asked Zoe enviously. She glanced at her heater, humming on the wall, and sighed.

Dad nodded. 'Sunshine every day. Your mother would have loved it here, Zo. Especially eating *alfajores*. Delicious!'

Zoe nodded, her eyes sparkling. She had seen her mum's handwritten recipe for *alfajores,* the caramel-filled cookies, slipped in between the pages of one of her old recipe books. An original recipe from Violette Picard was precious – and not just because she had been Zoe's mum. She had also been a world-famous pastry chef for the last twelve years of her life.

Dad cleared his throat. 'I miss you, Zo. I wish I could see you make those *fabulosas* cupcakes.'

'Me too,' said Zoe, feeling a prod of sadness in her chest. Coco rubbed her silky dark brown head on Zoe's cheek, tickling her with her whiskers. Zoe stroked her ears. Coco always knew how to make Zoe feel just that little bit better.

A crowd of people started pouring out of the building behind her father.

'What is that place?' asked Zoe.

'It's an old theatre,' said Dad, raising his voice slightly over the noise. 'It's been turned into a restaurant. I'm having lunch there today for my latest assignment.'

'What kind of food do they make?' asked Zoe.

'Seafood,' said Dad. 'They're famous for their fish dishes.'

Coco licked her lips, making Zoe laugh.

Dad smiled. 'I'd better go.' He adjusted his wig and glasses. 'I'll call again soon.'

Zoe nodded. 'Okay. Love you, Dad! Have a great lunch.'

'Thanks! Love you too, Zo. I'm proud of you for running your cake business all on your own. Not many kids could do that!'

'Thank you, Dad!'

He beamed and waved. 'Night night!'

Zoe waved Coco's tail at him. 'Night!'

She tapped the red phone icon and Dad vanished. She stared at the blank screen. Sunny Argentina sounded so good! Maybe Dad would take her somewhere on his next trip. But of course she had plenty to do at home. For Zoe wasn't an ordinary nine-year-old. She had a secret identity – she was Zinnia Jakes, the maker of fabulous cakes!

Zoe tapped on the ScreenTouch again to bring up the email she'd read that afternoon. She skimmed the most exciting bit.

Congratulations, Zinnia Jakes! We are thrilled to let you know that your entry, the Tumbling Tortoise Cupcakes, has been chosen to help celebrate our new endangered animals campaign. Keep an eye on our website – we are about to post the news!

Zoe felt a thrill whiz around her entire body. She nudged Coco. Her glowing eyes were fixed on the image of an elephant at the bottom of the email. Coco was tapping a caption under the elephant, using one claw like a tiny toffee hammer. Zoe read it aloud: 'Meet our new baby elephant, Chakrii!' She giggled. 'I'd like to meet him too, Coco. I love elephants.'

Aunty Jam poked her head around the door. She was wearing a long red dress with musical notes all over it. Zoe felt lucky that she was able to live with her aunt in her tiny cottage whenever her father was away. Jam was an amazing musician – she played the cello and also taught people of all ages.

'Time for bed, Miss Zoe!' she said, in her gentle voice. 'Did you tell Dad your news?'

'Yep!' said Zoe.

Jam came over and smoothed down Zoe's messy plaits. 'I was thinking that perhaps we should visit Wildside Zoo to meet the real Galapagos tortoises for extra inspiration. How about Saturday afternoon? Ben's playing at a café just around the corner. We could have lunch there first.'

'Oh yes,' said Zoe. She liked Ben, Jam's old university friend. He was a fantastic guitarist who often played in a duo with Jam.

'Great!' Jam said. 'We could take Addie with us if you like.'

'Excellent, Aunty Jam! Thanks!' Zoe leapt up and gave Jam a huge hug. She was the best aunty ever! 'Can I call Addie now? I haven't told her about my email yet!'

Jam shook her head. 'It's a bit late, Zoe. Tell her tomorrow at school instead. Hop into bed now.' Jam bent over and kissed Zoe on the cheek. She smelt delicious, like sugared violets.

'Okay, then,' said Zoe. She was bursting to tell Addie but she knew Jam was right.

'Try not to dream about tortoises and cupcakes all night,' said Jam. She pushed back her long dark hair and winked. She blew Zoe a kiss and left in a swirl of silk.

'I won't!' called Zoe. She plonked down her ScreenTouch on the desk and stood up, yawning. She pulled off her dressing gown, threw it on the desk chair and then settled beneath her duvet. Coco nestled on her stomach. Zoe made plans in her head for the next day. Even though Jam would be taking her to the zoo on Saturday, she needed to do a little more research on Galapagos tortoises so the cupcakes would be as perfect as possible. Tomorrow, she and Addie could hit the school library together!

Chapter 2

Zoe woke up the next morning later than usual. By the time she raced into the kitchen, her aunt was already putting bread into the toaster.

'Morning, sweetheart!' Jam sang. 'I was just coming to see if you were awake yet.' She sipped on her mint tea. 'What do you have on at school today?'

'Nothing special,' said Zoe, sliding onto a bar stool. 'We've got Art this afternoon. I've almost finished my tiger collage. I might be able to bring it home today.'

'I can't wait to see it!' said Jam. 'Oh, and talking about tigers reminds me of something. One of my students was telling me yesterday that his class had been invited by the zoo to go to the launch of the endangered animals campaign.' She put down her teacup. 'Did you know that some schools were going?'

'Yeah, Miss Wagner told us,' said Zoe, gobbling her toast. 'A big crowd of kids is going to make my secret delivery a bit tricky.'

'But not impossible,' said Jam, smiling. 'Zinnia Jakes can do it!'

After breakfast, Zoe brushed her teeth, grabbed her school bag and headed out the door, patting Jam's old blue and green van, named Beethoven, on the way. Beethoven transported Jam's musical gear to concerts, as well as acting as a storage unit for her spare cello case, and many other things she couldn't squeeze into her cottage. Beethoven also had another important function – he was the Zinnia Jakes secret delivery van!

Jam was slipping into the front seat, ready for a day of music lessons. Zoe waved as she zipped past.

'Later, Aunty Jam!'

Jam waved back. 'Bye, Zoe! Have a great day.'

Zoe took off down the pathway. Jam's house was a two-minute walk from school. *Tum-bling tor-toises*, she chanted in time with her panting breath and pounding feet. She couldn't wait to see Addie. She sped through the school gates, dodging the morning crowd of children, and burst into the classroom, causing Miss Wagner to raise her eyebrows. Zoe glanced at the clock. Three minutes until the bell. A new record!

'Hi, Zoe!' called Addie, from across the chattering, busy room. She had her maths book open on the desk that she and Zoe shared.

'Hi, Ads!' Zoe darted in between the rows of desks. Too many boys were milling around the last row, so she crawled under it.

She popped up and gave Addie the secret signal for a new cake order, making one hand into a claw shape and putting it on the top of her other hand.

Addie sat bolt upright. Her dark eyes were shining. 'Did you win?' she whispered.

Zoe nodded.

'Oh, that's fantastic!' She gave Zoe an enormous hug. 'I knew you could do it!'

The bell rang. Zoe threw her pencil case on the desk and sat down next to Addie. Normally when Miss Wagner called everyone's names at the start of the day, she looked bored. But today, Zoe knew something was up. She was beaming from ear to ear.

'Sit down quickly, everyone. Leon and Ryan, put the glue sticks down, please. I have some news for you all.'

'Bet it's not as exciting as yours!' Addie whispered to Zoe, giving her a mini low five.

Miss Wagner waited a few more moments as some late children straggled in and sat down at their desks. 'Well, I'm thrilled to tell you that our class has been invited to the Wildside Zoo for the launch of the endangered animals campaign,' she chirped. 'Isn't that wonderful?'

Zoe's mouth fell open.

Addie gripped her arm, hard.

'Ow!' Zoe yelped.

Miss Wagner tapped her foot. 'If you girls aren't interested in hearing about it, you can leave the room.'

'Sorry, Miss Wagner,' said Zoe. 'It's just that … I thought the zoo had picked which classes would attend the launch.'

'They had,' said Miss Wagner, peering over her glasses. 'But they rang this morning to say that another class pulled out last night. They asked if our class would like to go as their replacement.'

Chase whooped right in Zoe's ear. 'Yeah! A day away from school!' His friends laughed.

'Thank you, Chase,' said Miss Wagner crisply. 'I will only be taking those of you who know how to behave. This is an important occasion. Now, the only thing we need to worry about is a speech.'

'Speech?' asked Miranda, who was sitting in the front row.

'Yes. A class representative needs to report on how we hope to help endangered animals. I've decided that it should be our class captain, Polly.'

Everyone turned to look at Polly. She was the smartest person in the class, as well as the fastest runner. She won ribbons at every carnival. She could write really well too. *She was a good choice*, thought Zoe.

'Polly, this would mean a bit of hard work for you in the next few days,' Miss Wagner said. 'But I can help you if you're happy to do it.'

Polly's best friends, Katie and Yasmin, were nodding at her frantically.

'Yes, I'd like to do it,' said Polly, smoothing back her hair and beaming at Miss Wagner.

'Good!' said Miss Wagner. 'Come and see me after class and I'll let you know what kinds of things you need to speak about. Now, let's make a start on the day. Our maths test will be first.'

Zoe groaned. Uh-oh. She'd forgotten all about that. Almost everyone else looked glum too. Except Polly and Addie. Their faces had lit up, as if maths was fun or something!

During morning break, Zoe and Addie had a secret meeting behind the school hall.

'I can't believe our whole class is going to the zoo!' Zoe squeaked. 'My cake delivery is not going to be easy, Ads.'

'Can you do it?' asked Addie.

'I have to!' said Zoe. 'I can't let the zoo down.' She drew worried patterns in the gravel with her gingerbread girl shoes.

'I suppose it will depend on how easy it is to sneak into the zoo hall,' said Addie, frowning. 'Do you know much about it?'

Zoe shook her head. 'No. But Jam said she can take me to the zoo on Saturday. Do you want to come?'

'I'd love to!' said Addie. She skipped on the spot. 'I've only got gym on Sunday afternoon this weekend. We'll find a solution together. Besties, right?'

'Yeah!' Zoe beamed. 'Hey, can you come to the library at lunchtime with me,

Ads? I need a bit more information about Galapagos tortoises so I can get the cupcakes looking as real as I can.'

'Sure!' said Addie. 'These tumbling tortoises are going to be the best Zinnia Jakes creation ever, Zoe!'

Zoe smiled and nodded, even though she felt nervous – as if real tumbling tortoises were doing acrobatics in her tummy! She had never had to deliver a cake with all her classmates about. She twirled a plait around her fingers. Was this really going to work?

Chapter 3

When lunchtime came, Zoe and Addie wolfed down their sandwiches as quickly as they could. Then they headed to the library. The librarian, Mr Floros, was at his desk, watching a group of rowdy students with narrowed eyes.

'Does he know that our class is going to the zoo?' whispered Addie.

Zoe considered for a moment. Miss Wagner always seemed to be gossiping in the staffroom at break times, so it was highly likely. And if Mr Floros, or anyone else, saw them researching facts about tortoises, the Zinnia Jakes cover could be blown.

She shrugged. 'Have to assume that he does,' she muttered. 'We'll keep a good eye on him.'

'No-one's at the computers,' said Addie, pointing to the far side of the library. 'Let's start there.'

Zoe followed Addie over and they opened the online library catalogue. *Galapagos tortoise*, Zoe typed. Two books about the Galapagos Islands popped up. She and Addie found them quickly on the shelf right behind them. They took one each and began flipping through them.

'What exactly do you need?' asked Addie.

'As many photos of Galapagos tortoises and their habitats as I can find,' said Zoe. 'I have to get all the features and colours right for the cake.' Zoe ran her fingertips down the colourful page of the book she was holding. She liked looking at photos in books rather than using her ScreenTouch all the time – they seemed much more real somehow. She looked up at Addie. 'I like this book. There's lots of photos of the islands.' She snapped it shut. 'I'll borrow it.'

'There isn't so much in this one,' said Addie.

'No problem,' said Zoe. 'I …'

'Hi, Zoe. Hi, Addie.' Polly's narrow face suddenly appeared from around the bookshelf.

Addie gasped and dropped her book. Zoe turned hers over as quickly as flipping a pancake in a pan. She held the front cover tightly against her chest.

Polly gracefully bent down to pick up Addie's book. She pushed back her long hair, straightened up and passed it to her. 'Are you okay?'

'Fine, thanks,' said Addie. Her voice had a very un-Addie-like tone to it and Polly looked puzzled.

'I heard you guys talking about Galapagos tortoises,' she said. 'They're gorgeous, aren't they? Did you know that Zinnia Jakes is making tortoise cupcakes for the launch? I saw it on the zoo website.'

'Oh, really?' said Zoe. 'I didn't know that.' She swallowed.

'So how come you guys are reading about them? I'm the one doing the speech.' The puzzled look returned to her face.

'Oh, we know that,' said Addie. 'We just … well …' She gaped at Zoe with fear in her eyes.

Quick, think! thought Zoe. She looked at Addie's book. The cover showed a beautiful rocky island surrounded by crystal water. It seemed idyllic and relaxing … that was it! 'Addie's going on holiday to the Galapagos

Islands next term,' Zoe said. 'She was just showing me where she was going. We weren't really reading about the tortoises.'

'Oh,' said Polly. 'That's so cool! My cousins went there last year, so I've read all about the islands. Which ones are you going to?'

'I … I'm not sure,' said Addie. 'I'll have to ask Mum.'

Polly didn't reply. She was staring down at Addie, whose face had turned the colour of pillar box red icing. Then she fixed her blue eyes on Zoe and her book.

'Well, better go!' said Zoe, grabbing Addie's book and shoving it back on the shelf. 'See you in Art, Polly.'

Polly screwed up her nose. 'Urrgh. I wish I was as good at Art as you! That tiger collage you're working on is so good.' She looked again at the book clutched to Zoe's chest. 'Actually, I was thinking about asking

Miss Wagner if we should make some tiger stripe cookies to put on our fundraising stall for the zoo next week. What do you think?'

'Maybe,' said Zoe. 'I'm not so good at baking, though.'

'Really?' Polly sounded surprised. 'I can still remember that time in Grade 1 when we made biscuits with Mr Dunn. Yours were the best by far. My mum was helping that day and she still says she can't believe a six-year-old made them.'

'That was a long time ago,' said Zoe. She was glad Polly couldn't hear her heart pounding. 'I was much younger then.'

'Yes, I suppose so,' said Polly slowly. 'Well, see you after lunch.' She turned and walked away.

Zoe watched her go, then she turned to Addie.

Addie was looking horrified. 'You don't think ... does she ...?'

'I don't know,' whispered Zoe. Her arms were still clenched tightly around the book. Why had Polly been staring at the back cover? She slowly turned it around. The giant face of a Galapagos tortoise gazed serenely back at her. Zoe's heart fell like a badly made soufflé.

'Oh, Addie, how am I going to get away with this?'

Chapter 4

'Sorry, Coco,' said Zoe, for the fourth time on Saturday morning, 'but pets aren't allowed at the zoo.' She knelt down and prised Coco out of the cat carrier, which was sitting in the middle of the living room floor. Coco must have pushed it there all the way from its usual spot in the laundry. She usually hated going in it.

'Why do you want to go to the zoo?' Zoe asked.

As if in reply, Coco padded back into the carrier, then reversed out with something in her mouth.

'Hey, that's mine!' said Zoe, with a smile. It was a tiny toy elephant she'd had since she was a baby. She remembered playing with it with her mum. It always sat on her bed.

Coco stared at her and then dropped the elephant at Zoe's feet.

Zoe thought for a moment. 'Oh, I get it. You want to see Chakrii, the baby elephant. I'll tell you all about him when I come back home. How's that?'

Coco gave Zoe one of her most scorching looks.

'Meow, meow!' she said.

'Come on, Coco. You don't really want to go. There are wild animals there. They might scare you.'

Coco swished her tail and flounced off to the corner of the room, behind Jam's cello case. She wedged herself in so only the very tip of her tail was showing.

Zoe reached in to stroke Coco's back. Then the doorbell rang and she heard Jam open the front door.

'Hi, Addie,' Jam said warmly. 'We're all ready to go.'

Zoe snatched up her bubblegum cap and put on her strawberry sneakers.

'See you, Coco,' she said to the flicking tail tip. 'I promise I will tell you everything.' She smiled at her furry friend and then headed out to the hallway, where Addie and Jam were waiting.

'Hi, Ads!' said Zoe. 'Are you excited to go to the zoo?'

Addie nodded. She was hopping from foot to foot on the doorstep. The two best friends walked towards Beethoven while Jam closed the door behind them. She moved her amplifier and her spare cello case to make room for the girls, who climbed in.

She slipped into the front seat and started the engine. Beethoven roared to life.

'Have you thought about how you might deliver the cupcakes yet, Zo?' asked Jam, as they headed down the highway towards the city.

'No,' said Zoe, fiddling with her seatbelt. 'I've been too worried about Polly. But we're going to have to think of something good to hide seventy-eight cupcakes and get them into the zoo's hall without anybody seeing! They want them delivered by 12 p.m.

'That sounds fine,' said Jam. She looked at Zoe in the rear-vision mirror. 'I'm sure Polly doesn't really suspect anything.'

Zoe shook her head. 'You didn't see the way she looked at me – and then at the library book. What if she's worked it out? What if she tells everyone? It could be the end for Zinnia Jakes!'

'Let's take it one step at a time,' said Jam, guiding Beethoven into the middle lane. 'Continue to act innocent. Whenever Polly talks about cakes or tortoises, pretend you don't know what she is talking about.'

'But Polly's so smart!' said Zoe. 'I can't make one wrong move.' Her nerves were jangling as loudly as a drawer full of cake tins.

'Don't worry, Zoe,' said Addie, touching her arm. 'I know you can do it.'

'Yes, I'm sure it will work out, sweetheart,' Jam said soothingly. 'Now, who's ready for some lunch? The café that Ben's playing at is only a short walk from Wildside Zoo.' She pulled over and parked Beethoven on the street.

'Here we are,' she said, waving at the building in front of them. *The Zoo Café* was written in large zebra stripe letters over the top of one of the doorways.

Addie giggled. 'What a good name!'

Zoe laughed too and jumped out of the car. They stepped into the café. There was one table left and Zoe darted forward to claim it. In a dark corner was a tiny stage, where Ben was playing a soft relaxing melody. Zoe waved and he winked at them.

'I hear the veggie burgers are really good here,' said Jam, reaching for a menu. 'Oooh and they have lavender ice cream cones too! You should have one, Zoe – lavender's great for calming nerves.' Zoe nodded and smiled.

After a delicious lunch, she patted her full stomach. She felt much better. They said goodbye to Ben and walked towards the entrance of the zoo. It was a beautiful still winter's day with a hint of sun poking through the clouds. But the stillness didn't last. As Zoe made her way around the corner, she saw a long queue of people outside the zoo's iron gates.

'Goodness!' said Jam, stopping short. 'Hopefully it won't be as bad for the launch on Monday.'

Zoe gulped. The thought of a massive crowd of people was only adding more butterflies into her stomach!

Addie scampered off and came back with a zoo map. 'Maybe we can find out where the tortoises and the reception hall are while we are waiting.'

Zoe studied the map. 'There!' she said, jabbing her finger at the top. 'They're not far from each other.'

She followed Jam and Addie over to join the queue. When they had paid and were finally inside the gates, Zoe and Addie zigzagged through the crowd, holding hands.

'There are the Galapagos tortoises!' said Jam, pointing ahead to a fenced round enclosure.

Zoe skipped forward with Addie. They leaned over the fence, squeezing in among a row of small children. In front of them were two huge tortoises, both with wrinkled brownish necks and massive domed shells. They were eating from a pile of leaves. As Zoe watched, the larger tortoise raised its head and fixed its gaze on the children.

'Hi, tortoise!' said a small boy in front of Zoe.

Zoe glanced around. No-one seemed to be looking at her. She whipped her sketchbook out of her pocket and began to make some rough drawings. There were so many interesting patterns and colour shades on the tortoises' shells and their skin – *lots of possibilities*, she thought. And their eyes were stunning – black and glossy and wise. Their mouths were stained dark green from the leaves they were eating, so she made a note to include it on some of her tortoises.

Addie peeped over her shoulder. 'What flavour are the cupcakes going to be?' she whispered.

'I've planned to make chocolate and vanilla swirl cakes with lime icing,' Zoe whispered back, still madly drawing. She was holding the sketchbook as close as possible so no-one could see. 'Then I'm going to make marzipan tortoises in different positions on each cake, as if they are tumbling. Just for fun!' She quickly flashed the page to Addie.

'Wonderful!' said Addie, clapping.

Zoe smiled. They *were* good. The tumbling tortoises looked happy and mischievous. She stuffed her sketchbook back in her pocket. 'Let's check out the reception hall now.'

She pointed to a square brick building at the edge of the zoo. It had heavy glass sliding doors, taking up almost the entire front wall. Zoe raced over and pressed her nose up to them. It was a little hard to see inside with the sun glinting off the glass, but she could just make out a spacious room with stone pillars and a dark wooden floor. There were two long tables on wheels at the far end and rows and rows of chairs.

'Hmm,' said Jam, coming up behind them. 'I hope these glass doors aren't the only way to get in.'

'Not very sneaky, is it?' said Zoe, looking around. 'Everyone will be able to see me trying to make the delivery.'

'Come on,' said Addie. 'There must be another way.' She started down the left side of the building.

Zoe followed her. Lined up along the wall was a row of metal bins. Jam stopped suddenly.

'Look, there!' she said. She was pointing to a door that said *Staff Only*.

'Do you think it might be open?' asked Zoe. She heaved violently on the handle, making it rattle. 'No, it's locked,' she said.

But as she spoke, the door suddenly flew open, making her stumble backwards.

A bald man in a zoo uniform was glaring at her. 'Hey, what are you doing here?'

Chapter 5

'Oh, I …' Zoe stammered, flinching at the man's cranky expression.

'We were …' said Addie.

'I'm so sorry.' Jam stepped forward with her most winning smile. 'We didn't mean to do anything wrong, but could we come in this way?'

The man adjusted his name badge. *Max*, it said. His face looked slightly friendlier. 'No, you can't come in here. This is the side entrance to the reception hall. It goes to the backstage area. It's for staff.'

As he spoke, Zoe took the chance to peek in the doorway. She could see a small room with lockers along one side. There was a narrow space between the lockers and the wall. A long bench, cluttered with cardboard boxes, ran along the other side of the room. Zoe spotted two doors leading into the room – a black one behind the lockers and a green one right behind the man.

The man noticed her gaze and half-closed the outer door with his foot.

'Thank you, Max,' said Jam. 'Actually, my niece and her friend are coming here on Monday with their school and they are keen to look around.'

'Sorry,' said Max. 'As I said, only for staff.' He picked up a large bulging rubbish bag and stepped out of the doorway. The door closed behind him. He strode off towards the bins.

'Never mind,' said Jam, as they walked slowly back towards the front of the building. 'Maybe there's another way in.'

But although they walked right around the rest of the building, Zoe could only see a small, high window at the back.

'It's much too tiny to get a container of cupcakes through,' said Addie, shading her eyes.

'Yes,' said Jam. 'We'll just have to work on a cunning way to get you through that side entrance.'

'But how?' said Addie. 'We can't suddenly start working for the zoo.'

They began walking back towards the tortoise enclosure. Zoe stopped to see them again. They really were marvellous animals. Zinnia Jakes *had* to find a way to get those cupcakes delivered to the event.

The problem cooked in her head while they wandered around the rest of the zoo.

Zoe loved the butterfly house the best and was thrilled when one landed on her hat. Addie and Jam loved the tigers, and Zoe was proud to tell them some interesting facts she had learnt from making her collage. Just before they left, Zoe noticed the sign for the elephants. *Meet Chakrii!* the sign said. *This way.*

'Do you want to take a look?' asked Jam.

Zoe shook her head. After all, it didn't seem right to see the baby elephant without Coco. Besides, her feet were getting tired.

'I'm happy to go home, if that's okay, Aunty Jam.' A thought struck her. 'Actually, can we go to the gift shop first? I would like to get a few things if that's okay.'

'Sure!' said Jam.

The crowds were finally thinning out, so it didn't take Zoe long to find exactly what she was looking for at the shop. She paid with the money she got for her last birthday. Then she joined Jam and Addie back at the gates. They were chatting about all the animals they had seen, but Zoe could only think about her cupcake delivery.

'I just don't know how we are going to get in that door,' she said, as they went back to the car park and piled into Beethoven.

They drove off through the car park. Jam's phone rang through the car's media system. 'It's your dad, Zo.' She pressed the button on the dash. 'Hello, Ave. How are you?'

'Hey, Jam, I'm fine, thanks! Is Zoe there?'

'Yes … and Addie too. We've just been to the zoo.'

'Hey, Dad!' said Zoe, leaning forward.

'Hi, girls. How was the zoo trip?'

'Good … and bad,' said Zoe. She briefly told him everything that had happened.

'So you need a sneaky way in?' asked Dad. 'Let me help. You're talking to an expert!' Zoe could tell Dad was smiling. 'All you need to do,' he continued, 'is picture who might be at the event. Think about how you could blend in.'

'There'll be lots of students and teachers,' said Addie immediately.

'Waiters,' said Zoe.

'Technical people,' said Jam. 'Perhaps lighting and sound crew.'

'That's it!' said Dad. 'Those people need gear … some of which comes in large boxes, which would be …'

'Perfect for hiding cakes!' Zoe sat up in her seat. 'Great idea, Dad! We could pretend to be dropping off something for the tech crew.' She sat back and tapped her chin. 'Addie and I will be in our school uniforms, though, so people might not believe it. Maybe you need to do it, Aunty Jam.'

'I'm happy to try,' said Jam. 'Plus I've got a couple of black tech boxes at home for transporting my music gear. One's a bit old and battered, but it should be okay. We could easily fit a box of cupcakes inside each of them.'

'That's fabulous!' said Zoe. 'Thanks, Dad!'

'You're welcome!' he said. 'Glad I could help from so far away. Now, let me tell you about my lunch yesterday – it's a funny story!'

Zoe chatted to Dad almost all the way back to Addie's house.

'See you tomorrow for baking day!' Zoe called, as Addie scrambled out.

By the time Jam was pulling up at the cottage, Zoe was yawning. It had been a long day, but a successful one too. If only Coco had been able to come … she really wanted to see her. It didn't feel right that she hadn't been part of this so far.

Zoe clambered out of Beethoven and waited impatiently for Jam to get out the

house keys. 'Coco!' she called, as she burst
in the door. 'Where are you?'

Chapter 6

There was no answering meow, just silence. Jam put the car keys on the hallstand and her silver sandals neatly on the shoe rack. Zoe kicked her sneakers left and right.

'I might do some cello practice before dinner,' Jam said. 'Ben's asked me to perform with him next weekend and he's got some tricky tunes in mind! Maybe Coco is hiding because she's still upset with you.'

Zoe nodded. She peeped into the living room. No sign. Coco wasn't in the study or Zoe's bedroom either. That just left one place. Zoe went into the everyday kitchen and lifted up a crème caramel rug on the wall. Behind the narrow archway was her favourite place in the world – the Zinnia Jakes secret kitchen. It was as colourful as a giant fruit salad, with its rainbow cupboard doors and a long orange bench covered in tins of cookery tools and gadgets. Zoe could see Coco perched on the bookcase, staring out of the window at a few magpies on the lawn. Coco normally wasn't at all interested in wildlife. Zoe suspected she thought chasing animals was not worth the effort of moving even a single paw. If Coco was an ordinary cat, Zoe would have kept her inside. Luckily it wasn't necessary! It meant that Coco could help with cake deliveries. Except for this time.

Zoe tiptoed over to her and patted her back. Coco gave the very tiniest of ear flicks.

'Sorry you couldn't come today, Coco,' said Zoe. 'But take a look at this!' She held up a zoo gift shop bag, reached inside and unrolled a poster with a photograph of Chakrii on it. Coco didn't move.

'I bought you this too.' Zoe reached inside the bag a second time. She brought out a green silky scarf with elephants on it. Coco normally couldn't resist the feel of silk. She loved to snuggle in it.

Coco swivelled around and stared at the scarf for several seconds.

Zoe chewed her lip. This wasn't going well. 'And this too!' she said. She scrabbled in her pocket and pulled out the zoo map Addie had picked up at the entry gates. It seemed to do the trick. Coco jumped down and stroked her front paws over the scarf. Then she kneaded it like a baker dealing with delicate dough. Finally, she picked up the map in her mouth and placed it in front of her. She nodded slightly at Zoe and sat down, tucking up her paws. Zoe assumed that she had been forgiven.

'So glad you like them, Coco!' she said. 'Now, I really need your help! Would you be my model?'

Coco tilted her head to one side. Her whiskers quivered.

'I need you to be a tortoise. Can you pose in some different positions?'

In reply, Coco slipped the scarf over her head and struck an elegant pose on her side.

'That's great!' said Zoe, fumbling for her sketchbook. 'Let's try another one.'

Coco posed in several different ways, even adding a basket to her back that she fetched from the top of the bookshelf. Zoe sketched furiously. She modified each sketch into a Galapagos tortoise: each with its own shell pattern and deep black eyes.

By the time she went to bed that night, Zoe felt tired but also ready for the next day – baking day! Her very favourite part of being Zinnia Jakes. And she was so lucky that her bestie could help her! Addie had promised to be there bright and early.

The next day, Zoe woke just after sunrise and bounded out of bed. She was just tying on her Zinnia Jakes apron when Addie knocked at the door.

'Let's get cooking!' said Zoe, smiling at Addie's excited face. They raced each other into the Zinnia kitchen.

Zoe went straight to the pantry and fridge for supplies to make her very best swirl cake recipe. Everything was there – flour, sugar, butter, eggs, milk, vanilla and cocoa. She felt very organised, having bought all the ingredients she needed earlier in the week. By the time she had put everything on the bench, Coco had pulled out the right recipe book for her. Addie carried it over.

'Well done!' Zoe said, grinning. She plugged in her trusty red electric mixer and began to make the cake. When the batter was mixed to perfection, Addie helped her divide it evenly into two bowls.

'Now we need vanilla in one, and a dash of milk and cocoa in the other!' Zoe said.

As the cocoa-flavoured batter turned a rich dark brown, Zoe did a tiny tap dance and Coco wiggled her whiskers. *Perfect!* Zoe wiped her hands on her apron. Now it was covered in streaks of chocolatey brown.

'Addie, can you get out the cupcake tins, please?'

Addie clattered around in the drawer under the oven and pulled them out.

'Thanks!' said Zoe. She lined the tins with green cupcake cases and carefully spooned in dobs of each mixture. Then she handed Addie a skewer. 'You can swirl them together, Ads!'

'Sure!' said Addie. She made some beautiful geometrical patterns.

'Ready for baking!' Zoe cried. She slid the first three batches into the oven and banged the door shut.

'They should take about twenty minutes, Coco!' she said. 'Let me know when they're ready.'

Coco meowed wisely. She picked up the zoo map in her mouth, leapt back onto the bookshelf and laid it under her paws, her ears upright and alert.

'She just loves that map!' said Addie. 'I wonder why?'

'I think she likes the pictures of Chakrii,' said Zoe, dobbing in the next lot of mixture. 'I never knew she loved elephants so much. Maybe she's read a book about them!'

Jam came in a few moments later, dressed in her gardening overalls. 'Smells divine, Zoe!' she said. 'I'm just going to do some weeding out the back. Call if you need anything.'

Zoe gave her a thumbs up. She finished filling the last cupcake cases. While Addie swirled, Zoe collected up the dirty dishes. Then Coco leapt onto her shoulder from the bookcase and back again. She tapped her paws on the top shelf like an expert drummer.

'You're the best timer ever, Coco!' Zoe said. 'The cupcakes must be ready, Ads!'

Zoe whipped out a skewer and gently pierced a cake. It came out cleanly. Coco had got it right again! She put the next batches in the oven, feeling as light as a yummy chocolate mousse. Everything was going so well! She turned on the tap and squirted some dishwashing liquid into the sink. Addie started to put things away in the pantry.

Not long after, there was a knock on the front door.

'Ads, could you please see who it is?' asked Zoe, her hands in the sink. 'Jam must have locked herself out, but look through the peephole first.'

Addie nodded, leapt up and raced off, neatly lifting the rug to go through the archway.

Zoe hummed to herself as she began to wash the dishes. Coco mewed in time to her tune in between gazing longingly at her map.

A few seconds later, Addie appeared through the rug. She stood with her back against the kitchen wall, her eyes wide with fright.

Zoe gaped at her. 'Has something happened to Jam?'

Addie shook her head. She didn't seem able to speak.

'Then what's wrong?' Zoe stepped forward. 'Who was at the door, Addie?'

Addie leaned in towards her. 'It's … Polly!' she gasped.

Chapter 7

'Polly?' Zoe felt her jaw drop. 'What are you talking about?'

'I saw her through the peephole, and I opened the door because I thought I'd be able to get rid of her quickly. She's brought the tortoise library book with her.' Addie was stammering. 'I told her I'd pass it on, but she said she needed to talk to you. I didn't know what to do. She's waiting in the entry.'

'Okay …' Zoe tried to think clearly. It was strange that Polly would just drop in now. 'I'd better go talk to her or she might get even more suspicious.'

'You're right,' Addie gulped. 'But do you think you can get out of the Zinnia kitchen without her seeing you?'

'It's risky,' said Zoe. 'But I've got an idea.' She turned to Coco, whose ears were pricked up. 'Coco, can you sneak out and distract Polly? Keep her in the entry. You'll need to act as cute as possible.'

Immediately, Coco sped off to the doorway, poked her head under the bottom of the rug, wriggled her hindquarters and then darted out. Barely a second later, Zoe heard Polly's voice.

'Oh, hello, are you Coco? You're so cute. It looks like you're dancing! Would you like a pat?'

Zoe nervously checked the cupcakes in the oven. They were just done so she pulled them out. But would Polly be able to smell them? Her eyes fell on a bottle of Jam's home-made cinnamon and vanilla air freshener. Hopefully that would do the trick! She snatched it up and cautiously moved the rug aside. She tiptoed forward and peeked around the corner. Polly was stooped over, stroking Coco's back. Zoe sprayed the air freshener as quietly as she could, took a breath and quickly rounded the corner into the entry.

'Hi, Polly.' She sprayed a bit more air freshener for good measure. 'Sorry, I was just doing some housework for Jam.'

'Oh, hi, Zoe. That smells nice. I love vanilla.' Polly was still patting a purring Coco, who was twining herself around Polly's legs. Polly straightened and held out the book she was carrying.

'I noticed this was still in the library yesterday and I thought you might have forgotten to borrow it. It seemed to be important to you.' Polly's face was innocent, but Zoe wasn't buying it at all.

She shrugged. 'Oh, thanks, but like I said, it was for Addie. For her holiday.'

'Right. It's funny, though, because my mum is friends with Addie's mum, and she said she hadn't even mentioned a holiday to the Galapagos Islands.'

Zoe swallowed. 'Oh, really? Well, that's because …'

'Mum doesn't like to show off about holidays,' said Addie, coming up behind Zoe. 'She likes to keep them secret.'

'Hmm.' Polly was staring hard at Zoe. Zoe didn't like that at all. What was she looking at this time?

'Well, thanks for coming,' said Zoe, moving towards the door. 'I'll see you at school tomorrow.'

'Sure … by the way, that's a nice apron.'

'Apron?' Zoe's face went as cold as a fresh batch of ice cream. She looked down. She'd forgotten all about what she was wearing. Her apron was smudged with cocoa and ᵛilla cake mix. Even worse, it had 'Zinnia Jakes' on the pocket. It was a new product on the Zinnia Jakes website.

Zoe was starting to stammer an excuse when the front door squeaked open and Jam appeared.

'Oh, hello, Polly. I thought I saw you come down the driveway.' Jam flicked a glance from Zoe to Polly and back again. 'How is dinner coming along, Zo?'

'Dinner?' Zoe had trouble forming the word.

'Yes. It's great you are helping out, but I'd really prefer you didn't wear my apron.' She turned to Polly. 'I'm such a fan of Zinnia Jakes! It's a pity Zoe's not. She dislikes baking. Has she told you that?'

'Er, yes,' said Polly. 'But isn't that cocoa on your apron, Zoe?'

'Cocoa?' Jam laughed. 'No, it's gravy powder. Isn't it, Zo? I just hope you haven't made a mess of the kitchen while you've been making the vegetable soup.' As she spoke, Jam crouched down and stroked Coco. She seemed to be whispering something in her ear. A split second later, Coco bounded off down the hall. Addie glanced at Jam and followed her. Jam gave Zoe a quick wink. Zoe felt puzzled. What was she up to?

Jam smiled at Polly and smoothed down her overalls. 'Polly, would you like a quick drink and a snack before you go?'

'Thank you, Jam. I can only stay a few minutes, though. Mum's waiting in the car to take me to netball.'

Jam began talking about how she liked netball but loved music above everything.

All the while, Zoe stood frozen on the spot. What was Jam thinking, inviting Polly in? This was a disaster! Then Zoe heard clanking and shuffling sounds. They seemed to be coming from the everyday kitchen. What was Coco up to?

Jam finished talking to Polly and began walking to the kitchen. Zoe followed on wobbly legs. But as she entered the everyday kitchen, she had to stop herself from giggling.

Coco was sitting on the high bench, paws folded under her, looking as innocent as a lamb. A lamb in cat's clothing, that was! She was wrinkling her nose and licking her lips as if she was trying to get rid of a nasty taste in her mouth. Out on the countertop were the ingredients for vegetable soup – sticks of celery, a few carrots and three potatoes. Two more potatoes were rolling on the floor and there was a tin of gravy powder lying on its side next to them, with powder spilt all over the tiles. A tipped over carton of vegetable stock was pouring in a steady stream out of the open fridge. Zoe looked back at the bench. She might have been mistaken, but she thought she could see tiny toothmarks in the carrots.

'Zoe, what a mess!' said Jam, sounding stern.

'Sorry, Jam, I'd only just got started,' said Zoe. 'I'll clean it up.' She bent down to hide her smile.

Addie was placing a large pot on the stovetop. 'This is going to be great, Zo!'

'Do you like vegetable soup, Polly?' asked Jam.

'I don't mind it,' said Polly. Zoe detected a faint note of disappointment in her voice ... or was she imagining it? 'I think I'd probably better go after all. Thank you anyway.'

'No problem,' said Jam. 'I'll see you to the door.'

'Bye,' Polly said to Zoe and Addie. She looked again at the scene, shook her head slightly, and followed Jam out of the kitchen.

The moment Zoe heard the front door close, she turned to Coco. 'Clever girl! I'm sorry you had to drag all those vegetables up onto the bench. They mustn't have tasted nice to you. Were the potatoes the worst?'

Coco nodded firmly.

'Well, how about some tuna biscuits? You definitely deserve them.'

Jam came back into the kitchen. 'Whew!' she said. 'I think it might have worked, Zo. You were right – Polly is a tough customer! I'm not sure she's entirely convinced yet, but you all did very well.'

Zoe let out a breath. 'That was scary!' she said. She shivered. Polly had come way too close to discovering Zoe's big secret. She gave Jam a giant hug and Addie a high five. 'Thanks, everyone! Now, it's time to make those marzipan tortoises!'

Coco thumped her tail eagerly and Zoe laughed.

'Let's do it!' said Addie.

Chapter 8

Zoe was bubbling over with happiness as she walked to school the next morning. She had finished all the cakes the night before and they were perfect! She'd taken a photo straight away and sent it off to Dad.

Absolutely incredible! his message had said.

Addie and Jam had given her a round of extra-enthusiastic applause and Coco had jumped high in the air like a graceful sea lion! This had given Zoe an idea for how to present the tortoise cupcakes. She baked the leftover vanilla cake batter and made it into crumbs so it looked like beach sand. Addie had helped her pour it into a container, ready to sprinkle on the bottom of the two platters. Zoe skipped a few steps as she thought about her work. The marzipan tortoises, carefully shaped and painted with food colouring, were playfully tumbling about on the cupcakes, covered in various shades of lime green buttercream. She couldn't wait to see them laid out on the platters.

Zoe slowed her pace slightly. The only low point of the morning was that she hadn't got to say her usual goodbye to Coco. She had been hiding again. Zoe knew she was still a bit cranky about not being allowed at the zoo. She looked wistfully at the map every time Zoe and Addie talked about the delivery.

'You've tried to explain it to her,' Jam had said, as Zoe had poured out cat biscuits for Coco's breakfast. 'She'll come around eventually. Now, do you want to put the cupcake containers into my boxes before you go to school? They're with your cake supplies bag, ready for me to pack into Beethoven after I've finished teaching.'

Zoe had nodded. Jam had promised to take her and Addie to the zoo after she'd finished her morning cello lessons. Most of the other kids in the class were catching the bus from school.

'See you soon, tortoises!' Zoe had said. She'd blown the cupcakes a kiss and put the clear lids on top of her new eco cake containers. There was one large container and one small. Jam's black metal boxes were sitting on the floor, their hinged lids wide open.

When Zoe got to school, she found a sleepy Addie slumped on their desk.

'Sorry we finished so late last night, Ads,' she murmured, patting her arm. 'But everything's looking so good! Thanks for your help. Jam's coming to pick us up before break, so we arrive at the zoo earlier than everyone else.'

'Great!' Addie whispered, her face lighting up a touch. 'We should easily be able to keep the cakes hidden until we can deliver them, then.'

'Aren't you catching the bus to the zoo?' said a voice from behind Zoe.

Zoe tensed. Uh oh. Polly again. She turned, trying to relax her shoulders. 'No, Jam's taking us.'

'Why?' asked Polly, wrinkling her forehead.

'Well … um …' Zoe was getting sick of thinking up excuses every five seconds. Why couldn't Polly just leave her alone? An idea came to her. 'Jam has to do a cello performance near the zoo, so she said she would take us.' She nudged Addie. 'Isn't that right, Addie?'

'Yep!' Addie said.

'It sounds like you need to keep something hidden, is that what Addie said?' Polly studied Zoe closely.

'Hidden? Nope, you must have heard wrong,' said Zoe, hoping Polly didn't notice her shaky voice.

Polly nodded slowly and then wandered over to her desk at the far side of the room.

'Let's hope that's finally enough!' Zoe whispered to Addie.

The hour of school passed in a flash. Jam arrived right on time and soon Zoe and Addie were piling into the back of Beethoven, arranging themselves around Jam's spare cello case and amplifiers.

'Are the cupcakes all good?' Zoe asked anxiously, twisting around to see them in the boot space. She could see the two black metal boxes neatly stacked next to each other.

'They look great,' said Jam. 'So the only problem we've got now is trying to get in the side door of the zoo's hall. But I'm sure between the three of us we'll manage.'

Zoe crossed her fingers and kept them that way for well over half the drive to the zoo. She cringed at every bump in the road. But the solid black boxes stayed firmly in place. When they pulled into the car park, Zoe was relieved to see that there were no school buses in sight yet. She checked her watch. They still had an hour before the event to make the delivery.

Addie and Zoe jumped out and hurried around the back of Beethoven. Jam was hauling out a low flat trolley. It looked like a platform with wheels. Carefully, Zoe flipped open the larger metal box and looked through the clear lid of the cake container inside. Jam was right – the cupcakes looked fine. She breathed a sigh of relief as she closed the metal box. Jam helped her put it on the trolley. It probably wasn't worth checking the cupcakes in the other metal box. But Zoe just couldn't resist. She opened it and peeped into the second container ... the tortoises looked perfect! She pushed on the lid of the metal box to close it. Nothing happened. She pushed again. Still nothing.

'What's wrong?' asked Addie.

'I can't get the tech box to close,' said Zoe, rattling it. 'Something's happened to the hinges. The lid's jammed open! Oh no, everyone will see into the cake container inside!'

'Maybe we could bang the hinges with something.' Jam began searching among the jumble of musical accessories scattered around the boot.

But Zoe could already see there was nothing that could fix a set of broken hinges. Her palms were starting to sweat. Then she spied something.

'What can we do?' Addie was saying.

'Put the cake container in something else,' said Zoe. 'This!'

Chapter 9

Zoe pointed to Jam's spare cello case. 'The smaller cake container might fit in here.'

Jam stared. 'Let's try it!'

Addie stood guard as Jam opened the cello case. Zoe picked up the eco container and placed it inside. *Yes!* It just fit, although it was a tight squeeze. She closed the cello case, fastened up the clips and turned to Jam.

'We might need to change our story to get inside the hall. Could you say you're playing the cello at the event?'

'I can certainly give it a go. Great idea, Zo!' Jam picked up the cello case and laid it down on top of the big box. 'I've never transported a cello this way, but I can't put it upright or your tortoises really will be tumbling.' She grinned.

'Okay, let's do this!' Zoe pushed back her jelly baby headband and set off towards the zoo gates with determination. She and Jam pushed the trolley between them, each using one hand to steady the cello case. The ticket seller at the gates glanced at the girls' school uniforms and handed over free passes for the launch.

The zoo was far quieter today, but the few visitors who passed them gave them curious glances. Zoe tried not to look worried. She focused instead on Addie, just ahead of her. She was carrying Zoe's cake supplies bag, in which she had put the box of cake crumbs and the two cake platters. Her ScreenTouch was in the front pocket. Addie's shoulder was sagging and she definitely didn't walk with her normal springy steps.

She stopped suddenly. 'Your bag is sooo heavy, Zoe,' she groaned. 'I need a rest.' She set it on the ground.

Zoe frowned. What was Addie talking about? She was so strong from doing gymnastics! She could normally lift far heavier things than Zoe could. She left Jam with the trolley and went over to pick up the bag. It wriggled.

Zoe stepped backwards. 'Huh? What's going on?' The bag moved again.

'Maybe it's a rat!' said Addie, stepping back.

Zoe shuddered. She certainly hoped not. She grasped the top of the bag and gingerly peeped inside.

A pair of golden eyes gleamed out of the darkness. Zoe gasped. 'Coco!'

Coco gave Zoe a sheepish look, then retreated into the depths of the bag.

'Coco, you can't be here!' Zoe hissed. 'I told you cats aren't allowed at the zoo!'

Jam pushed the trolley up to her. 'What's wrong? Oh, Coco! She must have snuck into the bag just before I shut the boot this morning.' Her normally calm face was concerned.

'What are we going to do?' asked Addie in a panicked tone.

'She'll have to stay in the bag,' said Zoe. 'It's too hot for her in the car.' She peered back in. 'Coco, you'll have to keep quiet. No sudden moves. And don't rip the platter covers.' Zoe shook her head. Could anything else possibly go wrong?

They were now just steps away from the hall. Zoe headed for the side door. She and Jam stopped the trolley and Addie placed the squirming bag on the ground. Zoe took a breath and reached for the door handle.

She couldn't believe it. It was unlocked. She turned to Jam in triumph.

'Yes!' She pumped her fist in the air. Then she noticed dismay on Jam's face.

Zoe whirled back around. The door had swung open and there was someone standing in the doorway with folded arms. She gasped. It was the same man from the other day! He looked surprised, then angry.

'Not you three again! Clear off, or I'll call security.'

'Wait,' said Jam. 'I'm playing here today.'

The man regarded the cello case and frowned. 'You didn't mention that the other day.'

'It was a surprise for my niece,' said Jam, smiling sweetly. 'If you check, you'll know that I've been hired to play at the zoo today.' She reached into her skirt pocket. 'Here's my business card.'

The man took the card and looked at it silently.

'Please let us in,' said Jam. 'I need to tune my cello before I start playing.'

Zoe crossed her fingers behind her back.

The man stared at Jam for a long moment. 'All right. But you wait in the locker room while I go and find the manager. You'll need to speak to her about this.'

'Thank you,' said Jam. 'Give me a hand, girls.' She carefully picked up the cello case in her arms, turning sideways to get it through the door. 'The strap is broken,' she said to the man. 'Makes moving it around very difficult.'

The man didn't say anything. He just glared.

Zoe helped Addie push the trolley, with the box on top, over the doorstep. The wind picked up the door and slammed it shut.

'Wait here,' said the man. He stalked off through the green inner door, closing it behind him.

'Okay!' said Zoe, as soon as he disappeared. 'We haven't got long.' She turned to Jam. 'Jam, can you talk to the manager while Addie and I hide in here? Maybe you could tell her we left to see some more animals. We can sneak out to deliver the cakes somewhere in the hall once you've gone. I'm sure we can do it.'

'Of course,' said Jam. 'I'll take care of it. But where are you going to hide?'

'There!' Zoe pointed to the narrow space behind the lockers she had seen on their last visit.

'I think we'll just fit!' said Addie, checking it out. 'Great thinking, Zoe!'

They leapt into action. Zoe took the large cake container out of the black box, while Jam opened the cello case and Addie picked up the bag. Zoe heard a muffled mew from inside it as Addie put it over her shoulder and darted behind the lockers.

Zoe pushed the large cake container along the floor to Addie, then took the smaller one from Jam. Suddenly, she heard brisk footsteps coming from outside the room.

In a flash, Jam kicked both the cello case and the black box shut. 'Quick, Zoe, Addie, hide!' she hissed. 'I'll take the cello case and the box with me. When I get back outside, I'll hang around to alert you in case someone turns up. Good luck!'

Zoe gave her a thumbs up. She squeezed in next to Addie and pushed her back right up against the wall. It smelt musty and was such a tight fit she felt like she could barely breathe.

They waited, every muscle tensed. A second later, Zoe heard the green door creak open, followed by a cross woman's voice.

'What is going on here?' the voice barked. 'There are no musicians booked to play today. Why are you trying to get into the hall?'

Chapter 10

Zoe held her breath.

'Oh, hello,' said Jam smoothly. 'There must be some kind of mix-up. I'm booked to play at the zoo today. I'm replacing another musician who's ill.'

'That's not possible,' snapped the manager. 'There's only speeches, finger food and Zinnia Jakes cupcakes. No performers at all.'

Zoe's legs felt trembly at the mention of her cakes. She hadn't even delivered them yet! Addie squeezed her hand.

'How strange!' Jam said. 'The guitarist definitely said we were playing at the zoo. He even gave me the address. 528 Lion Drive. That's Wildside's address, isn't it?'

The manager broke into sudden laughter. Zoe and Addie looked at each other. What had Jam said that was so funny?

'Oh, dear me, I know what's happened,' chortled the manager. 'You're in the wrong place. You're supposed to be playing at The Zoo Café. That's their address. They often have live musicians.'

Clever Jam! Zoe grinned at Addie.

'The Zoo Café? Oh no! I'm not playing for the party? How silly of me! That means I'm running late. I'd better go.' Jam sounded flustered. 'I'm sorry to have troubled you.'

'That's quite all right. I'll see you out.'

Zoe heard the outer door open.

'Before you go,' said the manager. 'I thought Max said you had two schoolgirls with you. Where are they?'

Zoe's stomach tightened. She heard Jam stumble on the doorstep.

'Oh, they went back outside,' said Jam weakly. 'They're attending the launch with their school. I'll find them before I go. Thank you for your help.'

'You're welcome.' Zoe heard the outer door shut again. There were a few footsteps. Then the green inner door opened and closed. Silence.

Addie started to move, but Zoe held her finger to her lips. They waited for a few moments. Then Zoe sneaked a peek around the lockers. The room was empty.

'Okay, Ads,' she whispered. 'Let's check the doors.'

Addie went straight to the black door behind them, while Zoe scurried around the front of the lockers to the green door. She opened it slowly and gazed out into a long, dark hallway. There were voices coming from the left. She looked right. There was a red door at the end labelled *Rubbish Room*. Zoe wrinkled her nose and shut the door.

'This way's not good, Addie,' she said, scuttling back behind the lockers. 'What about your door?'

'Great!' said Addie. 'Come and see.' She was smiling. Zoe went over and looked through the open black door. She felt like cheering. There was another hallway, shorter this time. At the end was a door labelled *Kitchen*.

'Perfect!' Zoe squeaked.

Then she heard laughter from outside the green door. 'That was a tough morning's work!' a man's voice said. 'Time to go home.'

Zoe yelped. 'Let's go!' she whispered to Addie. They scooped up a cake container each. Zoe took the smaller one and grabbed Coco's bag too. She headed through the black door, let Addie through and closed it softly behind them.

'Almost there!' Zoe breathed.

She crept to the kitchen door and pushed it open slightly. In front of her was a small kitchen, lined with stainless steel benches. There were several trays of finger food laid out. But no-one was in sight. She gestured to Addie and they tiptoed in. Zoe put down the bag and reached in around Coco to pull out the platters. Addie helped her unwrap each one and set it on the bench. Then Zoe opened the cake crumb box and quickly scattered the crumbs on the platters. She placed the cupcakes gently on top. Coco watched everything silently, the top of her head poking out of the bag.

'It looks amazing!' said Addie.

Zoe beamed. She felt in her pocket for her flower tin, took out a red zinnia and placed it on top of one platter. Addie helped her put the eco containers and the cake crumb box into the recycling bin under the bench.

Zoe turned to Addie and gave her a high five. 'Let's get out of here!' Zoe pointed to yet another door, just in front of them. 'Hopefully this is the way out,' she said, crossing her fingers.

Zoe eased open the door. Four women in zoo uniforms were walking down the hallway. One was tapping on her phone and the other three were chatting to each other. Zoe closed the door quickly. After counting to twenty, she opened it again. This time, the hallway was empty. She put Coco's bag over her shoulder, then beckoned Addie to follow her. They stepped silently onto the carpet.

'Now,' whispered Zoe, 'we still need to be careful. We don't want to meet Max again. If we see anyone else, let's just say we are lost.'

Addie set her jaw and nodded.

They walked cautiously down the hall, dipping low as they passed a door with a pane of glass in the top. Coco wiggled every step of the way against Zoe's side, but she stayed quiet. Finally, the hallway turned a corner – and Zoe and Addie found themselves in the main function room. The room was buzzing with dozens of people in zoo uniforms, all scurrying about.

One man stopped them. 'What are you two doing here? You're supposed to be outside with your school group. That way!' He motioned to the glass doors. Zoe glimpsed a large crowd of schoolchildren in different uniforms milling around.

'Oh, thanks,' said Zoe, grinning.

'We're going,' said Addie. Then her face went pale. She clutched at Zoe's arm.

'Oh no, what now?' said Zoe.

'Our class is here,' wailed Addie. 'And there's Polly. Looking right this way!'

Chapter 11

'Quick! Over there!' Zoe grabbed Addie's arm and yanked her behind one of the pillars. She placed down her bag as gently as possible but Coco meowed crossly.

'Sorry! Just wait here one minute, Coco,' Zoe whispered. She peeked around the pillar. Addie was right – Polly seemed to be looking right at them through the glass doors. The girls half-waved at her. Polly didn't respond.

Zoe looked at Addie. 'It's okay, I don't think she can see in. The sun's reflecting off the glass.'

'Whew!' said Addie. 'Let's go and tell Jam we made it!'

'Just a minute,' said Zoe. 'I need to message the zoo.' She slid the ScreenTouch out of the pocket of her bag.

'I'll keep an eye on Polly,' said Addie, her eyes fixed in her direction.

Zoe began to type.

Your cakes have been delivered! You will find them in the reception hall kitchen. Zinnia.

'All done!' she said to Addie.

She knelt to put the ScreenTouch back in the front pocket. She stared. The bag was sagging on the floor …

'Oh no, it's empty! Coco!' she yelled. She jumped up and swung her head around, searching for a flash of brown fur.

Addie gasped. Her face went pale. 'What are we going to do?' She looked around wildly, then peered in the bag. Zoe saw her reach in and pull out something – a tattered piece of paper. It was a map. A very well-read zoo map.

'This is Coco's map,' said Addie, turning it around in her hands. 'Did you put it in here, Zoe?'

Zoe sucked in her breath. 'No, but I know who did. Coco! And I know why. She's gone to see Chakrii, the elephant, Ads. She must have been waiting for just the right moment to go.' She took the map and studied it. 'See? She's clawed out a "1". There's a "2" as well, right on the reception hall. She must be planning to come back when she's seen Chakrii. We have to go and find her.' She tried very hard not to imagine Coco slipping into the enclosure of some ferocious animal, but she couldn't help shivering.

She grabbed Addie's hand and was about to take off when someone tapped her on the shoulder.

'Hi, Zoe.' Polly's voice. Again!

Zoe turned. 'Hi, Polly. Sorry, but we've got to go.'

'Well … okay, but Miss Wagner just spotted you and asked me to get you and Addie.' She looked Zoe up and down. 'Are you all right?'

'Not really. Can't talk, Polly. Have to …'

'You have something important to do, right?' She leaned in. 'Zoe, I know your secret.'

'What?' Zoe felt a stab of horror. *Here it was*, she thought. *The end of Zinnia Jakes.*

'I know what you've been planning. You've brought Coco here, haven't you? I saw her running out a moment ago.'

Zoe stared blankly at her. 'Coco? Um, yes. You're right. But she's taken off! I have to find her!'

Polly looked concerned. 'Oh, Zoe, I'm so sorry. Let me help. Please.'

Zoe frowned.

'We could use all the help we can get, Zoe,' said Addie.

'Okay, thanks, Polly,' said Zoe, slowly. 'But don't you have to make your speech?'

Polly shook her head. 'Not for a little while. This is more important.'

Without waiting another moment, Zoe raced around the corner of the hall. There was Jam. 'Jam! Coco's disappeared!'

Jam put one hand to her mouth. 'What happened?'

'She's gone to see the elephants, Jam, I'm sure of it.'

'Okay.' Jam looked down at her cello case and the black box. 'I'm not going to be able to run with this.'

'Jam, why don't I stay here while you go and get Coco?' said Addie.

'Addie, you're the best,' said Jam. Addie smiled.

'Elephants are this way!' Polly said, pointing to the pathway on the left. Jam took off. Polly bolted after her, taking enormous strides that Zoe couldn't hope to match. But she did her best, gasping for air, going faster and faster, round one corner, and another, and another ... dodging people, leaping over rubbish ... then she pulled up short. There was the elephant enclosure, with a baby elephant standing right in the middle of it. Jam was bent over something at the fence. Polly skidded up to her.

Zoe charged towards them. 'Jam, is it ...'

Jam turned. She had something bundled in her arms. Something dark and glossy. Something shamefaced.

Jam looked relieved. 'She's fine, Zoe.'

Zoe breathed out. 'Coco! You really scared us.' She sighed. 'Did you like Chakrii?' Coco nodded, her eyes downcast.

Polly was right behind her. 'She … did she understand you? I don't believe it.'

'Yep!' said Zoe. 'She's one special cat. Just a naughty one, sometimes.' Coco purred contentedly in Jam's arms.

'Well, I'm so glad she's safe.' Polly fiddled with the hem of her skirt. 'Hey, listen, Zoe, I need to tell you something. I've been acting a bit strangely lately. That's because … um … I actually thought for a while there you might be … well … Zinnia Jakes!'

Zoe forced a laugh. 'Me?'

'Yeah. Stupid, huh?' Polly was blushing. 'But now I know you were only being secretive because you wanted to bring Coco to the zoo. And you weren't lying about Jam playing cello today. I saw all her gear. I'm really sorry, Zoe.'

'That's okay, Polly,' said Zoe. 'Let's forget all about it.'

'Thanks.' Polly smiled.

Zoe led the way back down the path. As soon as Addie came into sight, she waved madly and pointed to Jam's arms. She was hiding Coco under her flowing top. Addie beamed and sprang on the spot, almost knocking over the cello case.

'Polly!' Miss Wagner was fast-walking towards them. 'Where have you been? You need to go in now with the other student speakers.' She noticed Jam. 'Hello, Jam! Are you coming to watch the speeches? There's going to be Zinnia Jakes cakes too!'

'Really?' said Jam, glancing at Zoe. 'I'd love to come, Miss Wagner. It sounds fabulous!'

Chapter 12

'If I could have everyone's attention please
… thank you. Welcome to the launch
of *Out of Danger* – Wildside Zoo's new
campaign.'

'It's the manager from earlier!' Zoe said
to Addie with a wink.

The crowd, with its many schoolchildren,
broke into applause as a bright logo with
animal footprints appeared on the screen
behind the manager.

Zoe craned her neck to see the stage.
She, Jam and Addie had found seats in
the very last row just seconds before the

launch began. Zoe could see her class in the first and second rows. Miss Wagner had whisked Polly down the front, where she now sat next to five other students from different schools.

The manager adjusted the microphone and kept speaking. 'Three months ago, we asked schoolchildren like you to research endangered animals and come up with fundraising ideas to help them. And what a wonderful job everyone did! Six classes have been invited here today to represent children in and around our city.'

The audience clapped again.

'Now I'd like to ask a child from each school to speak to us about the work they have been doing. Our first speaker is Polly Schmidt from Mount Rumbling Primary.'

Polly stood and went to the microphone with a confident stride.

Addie nudged Zoe. 'When do you think they'll bring out the cakes?'

'Don't know. Right at the end, I guess.' Zoe's tummy was whizzing around like a milkshake maker, and she held the Coco-filled bag on her lap more tightly for comfort. It was open slightly and she could hear Coco purring loudly in a happy, fast rhythm. Zoe held a finger to her lips and Coco quietened back down.

When Polly started talking, Zoe forgot all about her cakes.

'Many people think that they can leave it up to someone else to make a difference to endangered animals.' Polly paused and scanned the whole audience. 'But that's not good enough. We all need to help. Donate your spare change to animal groups. Stop using plastic bags. Buy sustainable products. Reduce your water use. All these tiny things add up quickly. Tiny things make a big difference. Thank you.'

Katie and Yasmin cheered from the front row. Zoe clapped along with the audience until her hands throbbed. Hopefully people would love her tortoise cupcakes as much as Polly's speech!

When the last student finished speaking, the manager took over the microphone again. 'Thank you to our wonderful speakers and their important messages. Now, we have something very special to share with you all. What's a celebration without food?'

Zoe clutched Addie's hand. This was it!

She watched closely as a group of zoo staff members wheeled over the two long tables. On a count of three, they whisked off the tablecloths. One cake platter was on each table. Coco's head raised slightly out of the bag. A huge photograph of the tortoise cupcakes was beamed up on the screen behind the manager. There were gasps and murmurs from the crowd.

'Take a look at these tumbling tortoise cupcakes, made by the one and only Zinnia Jakes!' continued the manager. 'They were delivered mysteriously just a short time ago. We have no idea how she achieved it. Zinnia has made Galapagos tortoises – the first animal our campaign is going to focus on. Thank you everyone for coming and enjoy the cakes!'

Zoe beamed as the audience got to their feet. She looked into the bag. Coco's eyes were soft. She put her paw on Zoe's hand.

'Thanks, Coco,' Zoe whispered.

Jam reached over and patted Zoe on the back. 'Well done, sweetheart,' she said quietly.

Zoe handed the bag to Jam and then she and Addie wriggled their way through the crowd down to the tables. The cupcakes were going fast! Zoe felt pride warm her whole body. She couldn't wait to tell Dad later on.

'One cake each, please,' the manager was saying to the queue of children at the platters. She was cradling a cupcake of her own, topped with a tortoise with its hind legs in the air. 'Oh, these are just delicious!' she said to a group of teachers standing nearby, who were all exclaiming over the tortoises.

Polly appeared next to Zoe. Her lips were smeared with green icing.

'Great speech, Polly,' said Zoe. 'Congrats!'

'Thank you,' said Polly, wiping her mouth with the back of her hand.

'Was the cupcake yummy?' asked Zoe.

'It was the best cake I've ever eaten!' Polly exclaimed. 'The tortoise looked exactly like a Galapagos one. Zinnia Jakes is so clever!'

She put a finger to her lips. 'You know, I think she must be the pastry chef at that fancy French restaurant my parents love. She's the best! But do you think it's difficult making and delivering cakes in secret?'

'Probably,' said Addie, smiling at Zoe, 'but it must also be pretty exciting. Don't you think, Zoe?'

'Definitely exciting,' said Zoe, grinning back at her best friend. 'And sprinkled with a lot of fun as well.'

Turn over
the page for
an exciting
cake recipe!

Zinnia Jakes's Secret Recipe File:

Chocolate swirl cupcakes

(Makes 12)

Hey, everyone! I'm Zinnia Jakes. Here is my secret recipe for chocolate swirl cupcakes – they are delicious! And remember, baking should be mixed with merriment, whisked with wonder and iced with inspiration!

Note: Make sure you ask an adult to help with putting aside the ingredients and the baking, especially when you need to use the oven.

★ For the cupcakes, you will need ★

- ♥ 1 ½ cups self-raising-flour sifted
- ♥ 125 g butter, chopped, at room temperature
- ♥ ⅔ cup caster sugar
- ♥ 3 eggs, at room temperature
- ♥ 1 tsp vanilla essence
- ♥ ¼ cup cocoa, sifted
- ♥ 1 tbs milk
- ♥ Cupcake cases
- ♥ A 12-hole cupcake or muffin tin
- ♥ An electric mixer
- ♥ Two large bowls

★ For the lime icing, you will need ★

- ♥ 125 g butter, chopped, at room temperature
- ♥ 1 ½ cups icing sugar, sifted
- ♥ 2 tbs of milk
- ♥ A few drops of green food colouring
- ♥ An electric mixer
- ♥ A large bowl

★ Instructions ★

1. Preheat the oven to 180 degrees Celsius and line the tin with the cupcake cases.

2. Beat the butter, sugar and vanilla with the electric mixer until it is creamy. I always test it at this stage to make sure it is *vanilla-y* enough. You can add a little more if you like. Yum!

3. Add the eggs one at a time, beating well after each one.

4. Add the flour and the milk. Beat on a low speed until everything is mixed together.

5. Pour half of the mixture into the second bowl. (It doesn't need to be exact, though if you have a friend as precise as Addie, it probably will be!) Add the cocoa powder and the milk and mix them gently into the batter with a spoon.

6. Now comes the tricky part! Put one tablespoonful of vanilla mixture into each cupcake case. Top it with a tablespoonful of the chocolate mixture. Keep going until each case is about ¾ full.

7. Here's your chance to be an artist! Use a skewer to lightly swirl the mixture in each cupcake case. This is so much fun. Warning: Don't go too crazy or you won't get a nice swirled effect.

8. Bake the cupcakes for about 20–25 minutes, or if you have a cat, until it lets you know it is time. ☺ While they are baking, you can make the buttercream icing. Use the electric mixer to beat the butter until it is pale. Add half of the icing sugar and beat well. Then add the other half, the milk and the food colouring all together.

9. Now you have to let the cupcakes cool. (Trust me on this. If you don't, you end up with crumbs in the icing, which is not fun.) Then you can use a blunt knife to ice them.

10. Top your cupcakes with whatever you like! It doesn't have to be tortoises. (But if you want to do this, you can make them from ready-rolled fondant and colour it with food colouring.)

★ **Enjoy your swirly cupcakes!** ★

Read an extract from

The Fabulous Cakes of
Zinnia ✲ Jakes

The Crumbling Castle

Chapter 1

The best cakes I've ever eaten! They must be the work of The Genius Chef.

Magical! Is this some type of witchcraft?

Her cakes are out of this world! But please answer me this. Who is Zinnia Jakes???

'Zoe! Pay attention!'

Zoe slammed shut her ScreenTouch and tried to slide it under her spelling book. But it was too late! Miss Wagner's beady eyes were extremely sharp. She was already swooping down.

'Is that a ScreenTouch?' she asked, thrusting out her hand. She made it sound like something that tasted disgusting.

Zoe shook her head, then gave up and handed it over. Miss Wagner flipped open the cover and tapped the screen with a tangerine fingernail. She peered at it.

'This is supposed to be a maths lesson, Zoe. Look at fairy cakes in your own time!'

The kids in the row behind Zoe laughed. One kicked her chair. She didn't even have to turn to see who it was. It was *always* Lucas. He'd called her 'Freckle Face' on her very first day of school and had been annoying her ever since.

Miss Wagner was taking the ScreenTouch back to her desk. 'Besides,' she said, 'cakes are full of sugar and very bad for you!'

Zoe said nothing. She happened to know that her teacher had a Zinnia Jakes cake box in the staffroom fridge. It had been delivered for Miss Wagner's birthday that very morning. Her sister had ordered her two pink fairy cupcakes at 6.46 p.m. the day before. Zoe knew this because Zinnia Jakes was not a TV chef, nor a witch, nor even the world's greatest magician. Zinnia Jakes was a nine-year-old girl. Zinnia Jakes was Zoe Jones.

Zoe only realised she had a talent for baking two years ago, on her Aunty Jam's birthday. On that day, she'd woken up with a picture in her mind as clear as shards of sugar glass. She would make a surprise birthday cake for her aunt. She'd just read a book about exotic birds so it had seemed a good idea to make a cake in the shape of an emu. The legs and neck were made of chocolate mousse and the rest had been a beautiful rich hazelnut sponge cake. Zoe had barred her aunt from the kitchen and spent all morning on it, even ruffling up the icing to make it look like shaggy feathers. Jam had almost tripped over her music stand when Zoe had brought out the cake. And when her aunt had tasted it, she'd reached out for Zoe's hand and said it was the most glorious cake she'd ever eaten – as delicious as any of Zoe's mum's creations.

Zoe had wished her mum was still alive to hear that. Violette Picard had been one of the most famous pastry chefs in the world.

Then Jam's fork had clattered onto her plate. She'd had a fabulous idea: Zoe could start her very own cake-making business!

Right away, Zoe had frowned. 'But who would buy cakes from a kid?'

'We won't tell anyone who you are,' said Aunty Jam. Her hand had strayed to the hot-pink flower in Zoe's hair, a zinnia, freshly picked that morning. Jam had waved it like a magic wand. 'We'll sprinkle the business with mystery … you can have a secret identity!'

'Like Dad?' Zoe felt fizzy bubbles rising in her stomach from excitement. Her dad's job as an international food writer was top secret. He had to visit restaurants all over the world to taste and write about the food – usually in disguise. He'd fallen in love with Zoe's mum in a restaurant in Paris after she'd presented him with one of her extraordinary desserts.

Jam had laughed. 'Yes. Like your dad. Or a spy … one who works undercover to bake and deliver cakes. Let's do it, Zoe! First, we need a name for you and your fabulous cakes, something with a lovely rhythm …' She'd stared at the zinnia in her hand and snapped her fingers. 'I've got it!'

And that was how Zinnia Jakes had burst into life.

Zoe smiled to herself and spun her pencil between her freckled fingers. She still felt butterflies in her stomach when she thought about her baking adventures. Then she realised Miss Wagner was glaring at her and she quickly bent over her work.

When the home-time siren went, Zoe went straight to Miss Wagner's desk.

Miss Wagner rapped her fingers on the ScreenTouch. 'Zoe, this is just not good enough …'

The same words as always. Zoe tried not to yawn. She pretended to listen to Miss Wagner's stale lecture. Then she took the ScreenTouch, yanked up her jellybean socks, grabbed her bag and charged straight out to see her best friend, Addie. She was practising handstands in the playground in her usual spot. Even though plenty of kids were pushing past her, she still managed to keep her balance. She was a superstar!

Zoe waited for Addie to turn back up the right way. She thought about her baking schedule. Miss Wagner's cakes had marked the end of a busy two weeks. *What would turn up next?* She sighed. There were only so many teddy-bear and fairy cakes one could make without getting bored. She hoped a new challenge wasn't far away!

★ ABOUT THE AUTHOR ★

Brenda Gurr adores anything to do with spies, adventure and mysteries, so writing a book about someone with a secret identity is something she has always longed to do. Add to that her love of cats (she owns two magical Burmese cats) and her habit of baking far too many sweet treats, and you have all the ingredients for the world of Zinnia Jakes! A former storytelling fairy, drama teacher and school worksheet writer, Brenda is the author of numerous books for children. This is her first chapter book series.